BEAUTIFULLY
BROKEN

JACK KEETON

Cover photo: Sarah Clarke Photography
Facebook.com/SarahClarkPhotography2014

Cover Design by: Zeljka Kojic

ISBN: 979-8-9897243-0-7 (paperback)

DISCLAIMER:

This is a work of fiction. Character names and descriptions are the product of the author's imagination. Any resemblance to actual persons, living or dead, is entirely coincidental.

Dedication

To my beloved Sylvania

Acknowledgments

It is impossible to thank everyone responsible for *Beautifully Broken*. If I must acknowledge one person who made it possible, it would have to be my beloved Sylvania. Without her constant guidance and loving presence, I would not be here.

I can't overlook the one who never got to meet her and shares the same magic that set her apart: my grandson, Teddy. Through his eyes, I could see what life would have been like without poverty and violence.

ACKNOWLEDGMENTS

I can see myself in him as Sylanvia saw herself in me. Someday, when Teddy reads this book, I hope he realizes many journeys created the path he finds himself on.

Table of Contents

Prologue

My memories begin before my feet hit the dirt road, running from the hell I was about to enter. I can see my beloved grandmother Sylvania before my birth, draining the last bit of her strong, bitter coffee so she could see the grounds at the bottom of her cup. Since her first sip of coffee as a little girl, Sylvania has been able to see the future in coffee grounds.

She had a talent, though it didn't take anyone with talent to see what she saw. She looked up at her daughter, my mother, Virginia, and said, "This young'un is gonna get drug down a long dirt road." I sat heavy in Virginia's belly, stretching my foot out so it could be seen through her tight t-shirt.

"This baby is going to see the rain. Oh, it's going to storm on his head." My beloved Sylvania grasped her daughter's cracked hands. She laid her hands on Virginia's belly and began speaking in a tongue only my angels and I could understand.

In that special language, she said [in translation], "I pray God's favor on this child. Lord Jesus Christ, surround him with light and love. Mother Earth, summon the wind to blow away this storm."

Sylvania's hands moved over the last comfortable home I would know for years—my mother's stomach. "I place a hedge of protection on this child. I summon God's energy and power and use it to glorify this child of His creation."

"Mama, God don't like witchcraft. It says so in the Bible, and I don't like you using it on me."

"God don't like no-account men, neither, but you hang on to yours. It ain't witchcraft, anyway. Witchcraft is the devil's power. This is God's power and energy, and He gave me the Gift to summon it to glorify Him."

Mama rolled her eyes at her Mama. She pretended not to believe in her mother's power, but we all knew there was something to it.

Chapter One

Just as Sylvania had predicted, it stormed that April night I was born. It was 1960, and in the very primitive area where we lived in Ohio, the part the locals called "little Kentucky," most women gave birth at home. Two hundred miles away from the woman who protected her and her baby, Mama had no transportation. Daddy was out who knew where probably drunk. Mama muttered, "He's probably laid up in some whorehouse, out spendin' my baby's grocery money."

Mama already had six children, and she sent her eldest a mile down the road to fetch Miss Bessie, who wasn't officially a midwife but had helped a lot of the local women get through the worst of it in their own beds. Miss Bessie hadn't delivered Mama's other children. They'd all been born in different places on account of how my Daddy couldn't keep a home for us to live in for very long. At this time, we were staying with Daddy's mama, my Grandma Ruby. Grandma had gone to visit her daughter Garney Fay, who was also pregnant and having a hard time of it. She had promised to be home before I came. I wasn't due for another three weeks, and Mama always delivered late.

Not this time. My eldest brother went to fetch Miss Bessie, running down the muddy road barefoot, hair plastered by the rain to his scalp. He was only nine, but Daddy's constant hard knocks had made him a man. He returned sooner than anyone expected, sitting in the bed of Miss Bessie's truck, washing all the mud off himself in the rain.

Miss Bessie took one look between Mama's legs and said, "Oh no, child. We got to get you to the hospital."

Mama had never been to the hospital. My siblings had all been born at home in whatever bed or pallet she was lying in. Between contractions, Mama asked, "How am I gonna get there? How am I gonna pay for it?"

"Never you mind all that," Miss Bessie said. "I'll take you in the truck."

"I ain't got no money to pay."

Miss Bessie snorted a laugh through her nose. "Ain't no one around here got no money. They's used to it. But they ain't gonna let you or the baby die, which is what's gonna happen if you don't let me take you to the hospital."

Mama didn't much care for her own sake if she died, and she might have thought it was a blessing if I did – one less mouth to feed, one less squalling baby to contend with. But she knew that my siblings wouldn't survive without her, so she agreed. Besides, if hospitals were anything like she had seen in the movies, it would be a vacation. She'd lie on clean sheets, with meals brought to her on trays and kindly nurses seeing to her every need.

When she got to the hospital, the doctor agreed with Miss Bessie—I was stuck. As a trickle of blood ran down Mama's thigh, he wheeled her into an operating room and prepared for a C-section. Before he did, a nurse, who had taken a sort of history from Miss Bessie, whispered that I would be her seventh child and Mama would be a charity case.

The doctor took it upon himself to see that Mama wouldn't have any more children. I suppose Mama ought to have been mad that no one asked her, but she was more grateful than anything else. Not yet thirty, she was done having children. She loved us, but we were all too much. Besides, the operation gave her another day of lying in that comfortable hospital bed.

Dr. Showers meant well and was a good man. He took care of Mama and all of us children, knowing he wasn't likely to get paid much if anything at all. It wasn't like he needed our money, anyway. He built himself a huge mansion uptown. I would stand in front of that house wondering what kind of life you had to live in order to own a house like that. I guess I figured it out because that's where I raised my children.

A lot of women died during childbirth in that part of the world. I suppose Mama might have, too, if Dr. Showers hadn't taken over when he did. I ran into him one evening a few years ago. My wife and I were going to dinner. We walked into the elevator. The restaurant was on the 30th floor, so we had a minute to ride. A man stopped the closing door with his arm and stepped into the car. I knew him immediately. We locked eyes, and he said, "Are you one of the Keeton kids?"

"Yes. I'm the youngest."

"Is your mother still alive?"

"Yes, sir."

Dr. Showers shook his head, a big grin splitting his face. "I'd imagine she is. If Noble Keeton didn't kill her, death might have a fight on his hands."

Mama had barely made it back to Ohio when the labor pains came for my birth. She had gone back home to Kentucky for my cousin Jackie Lynn's funeral. Mama's sister, Alice, brought Mama and all her children down in her brand-new Cadillac. Alice didn't stay for the funeral, though. Aunt Alice wasn't like my Mama. Alice was a wild cat. "Why go to a funeral when there's living to be done?" she called out the window of her shiny Cadillac. "There's folks who need to see this car my new husband bought me." Most folks thought she had moved to New York City not long after that, but no. She was laid up in some sanitarium recovering from a case of syphilis that nearly killed her.

Just a few weeks before I was born, my Aunt Wanda had a little girl she'd named Jackie Lynn. Jackie Lynn howled like a banshee with her first breath; they all said it was a good sign. But good sign or no, Jackie Lynn didn't live a whole week before they had to bury her in a tiny graveyard out behind Grandma Sylvania's house.

Now, I was born and needed a name. Since Aunt Wanda didn't have any babies to take care of, she came to take care of my brothers and sisters while Mama was lying in that hospital bed with the starched white sheets. Mama was so grateful she asked Aunt Wanda what I should be named. I suppose she felt it was an honor, but mostly, Mama was tired of thinking up names.

Aunt Wanda looked at me, wrapped up tight in a hospital blanket, and said, "He's a purty little thing."

"He's a boy, Wanda. Boys ain't purty."

"Well, this one is. He's a looker. He looks…" Aunt Wanda wiped away a tear. "I think God gave him my baby's soul. So I'm giving him my baby's name. This here's Jackie Lynn."

And that's how I got my hand-me-down name. Everyone deserves their own name. I wasn't even set aside by a 'junior' or a 'third.' I was just given a name that had already been used. Jack was a common enough name, and there were a few boys around named Lynn, but that didn't stop the nurse from checking 'female' on my birth certificate paperwork.

We didn't figure out what happened until Mama tried registering me for school. It took a lot of paperwork to sort that out. By that time, my eldest brother, Charlie, was fifteen, and he thought that might be the funniest thing he'd ever heard. He convinced all the other kids that I'd been born a girl, only Mama wanted a boy, so she had me switched, and that's why I had a girl's name. Mama swatted him when she heard him say that. "Now, Charlie, you know that ain't true."

But he'd just say, "Then why's his birth certificate say he's a girl?" And by then, Mama would be off doing whatever came next on her endless list of chores.

Chapter Two

Daddy's name was Noble, which was a joke if God ever made one. Just like the man down at the grocery store who worked in the meat department. He was so big he broke a sweat carrying a steak from one end of the store to the other. The only name I ever knew him by was "Slim."

Slim was a nice man. He caught me rummaging through the dumpster once. "What are you looking for, boy?"

I wiped my dirty hands on my pants and hung my head. I would have run if I could, but I had managed to climb into the dumpster and wasn't sure how to get out. I didn't know if stealing out of a dumpster was regular stealing and if I'd go to jail, and I was ashamed. "I'm hungry," I said. I couldn't think of anything else.

Slim looked down at me. He was a big man, big enough to dwarf most of the grown men I knew, but I was five years old and only about three feet tall. Even with the extra height being in the dumpster gave me, it felt like I was Jack from the nursery rhyme, looking up at the giant from the beanstalk.

Slim reached into the dumpster and lifted me out with one arm. "You stay right here."

Now that I was out of the dumpster, I could run but was afraid. Slim surely knew who I was, and running would just delay the punishment I would likely get. Might as well face it and get it over with.

Slim came back in less than a minute, a package of pecan cinnamon rolls in his meaty hand. He held them out to me, but I just stood there. Was Slim rewarding me for stealing?

"Go on," he said. "Take it."

"Thank you, Mr. Slim, thank you. Please don't tell my Daddy what I did. He'd be so angry."

Slim narrowed his eyes and took my measure. "You ain't got nothing to worry about with your Daddy on my account. Can't say nothing about his account, but this is just between us. Don't you tell nobody neither."

He walked back into the store, and I sat right there next to that dumpster and ate the entire package.

I went back to the dumpster pretty regularly after that. I don't know how Slim knew when I was coming, but he always had something for me sitting on some old wooden crates in the back of the store. It was usually some pastry—the kind I would never get at home. I felt guilty eating them, thinking those beautiful pastries were meant to go to a beautiful home with the perfect family instead of to me with my grubby hands. I made a promise to myself that someday I would have the kind of life this beautiful pastry belonged to.

* * *

Daddy was a hell of a stone mason when he was sober, which might have been two or three days out of the month. Just enough to keep us from starving but close enough to starving to see it clear on the horizon. He always seemed to work but never had any money; whores, poker, and liquor took care of that. It got around that Noble was the best stone mason around, and as long as he wasn't whoring or drinking while he worked, no one cared.

Daddy's hands were always calloused, his fingernails filed down from the cement, and his skin so tough you could drive a two-penny nail into his thumb, and he wouldn't even feel it. Maybe because he was so tough, he thought the rest of us were, too.

Once Mama got done living the high life in the hospital after I was born, she went back to her regular life, where no one brought her anything but grief. She'd been happy to stay the extra day, and Lord knew she didn't want any more children, but she realized something hard when she got home. Daddy wouldn't hit her when she had a baby in her arms.

That's probably why I didn't learn to walk 'til I was two. There wasn't any need. Mama never put me down.

My beloved Sylvania once told me that empathy was a gift. She said there was something special about being able to feel the feelings of the people you loved. But it didn't feel like a gift to me. Whenever Daddy got to yelling, Mama would grab me up and hold me close.

"Noble, hush," she'd say, stroking my hair. "You're scaring the baby."

"He ain't a baby no more," Daddy growled as Mama kissed the top of my blonde curls. My brothers and sisters would scatter at the first sign of trouble, but I was always trapped there, being a shield for Mama.

I could feel her fear. It came off her in waves. She would pet me and make soothing sounds, but even then, I knew she was trying to soothe herself. I wanted to run out in the woods with Charlie or hide under the bed with Kathy, but I couldn't go anywhere with Mama gripping me tightly.

So, I learned how to disappear inside my own head. Playing peekaboo with Mama, I figured no one could see me as long as my eyes were closed. I'd close my eyes, bury my face in Mama's chest in case my eyes flew open on their own accord, and visit my beloved Sylvania.

I don't know if Sylvania ever knew I came to visit her, but I loved those journeys. A loving presence always accompanied me. Who else would that be but my beloved Sylvania? In that hideaway, I felt safe. I understood a language that had never been spoken before and heard songs that hadn't yet been composed. I saw colors that weren't on the spectrum. It was my special place. I spent a lot of time there, deep inside my own head, completely unaware of the poverty and chaos around me.

I know now that I had learned to disassociate at a young age. I couldn't have been more than two or three. But instead of separating from myself and feeling divided, I felt whole. I knew I was safe there. I knew my beloved Sylvania would shelter me. I could feel the hedge of protection she'd placed around me before I was born.

By the time I was four, I could control that space. I could dive in whenever I wanted to, whenever the world was a place I didn't want to be. In the physical world, I found a hidden door in the back of the linen closet that led to a hollow underneath the stairs. I loved the complete darkness. I could go to my secret space in the house with my beloved Sylvania. I was doubly protected.

The older I got, the more time I spent under the stairs. It was my Holy of Holies. Being the smallest and weakest in such a large family, hours would go by without anyone realizing I was missing. By the time I was four, I was too big for Mama to snatch up when Daddy got to yelling, but I was still too small to do anything about it. So, I'd disappear into the darkness where I didn't have to work to keep my eyes shut. Instead, I could gaze beyond the darkness into the world I'd created.

This world was truly another world. Looking back, I'm not sure how a child of such a tender age could create such a magical, majestic universe. I knew how Danel felt in the Lion's den and how Shadrack, Meshach, and Abednego felt after being saved from the furnace by God. Nothing could touch me.

Mother had a specific wail that was like an air raid siren. It told us to take our positions; bombs were about to drop. When we heard her screaming, we all ran in different directions. No matter which way we started, we ended up together, running barefoot through the wet weeds in the dark. If Noble was able to snag you, Heaven forbid, you would be stuck sitting and listening to him rave until he passed out. Sometimes, he started fighting with his own father, who was around a lot. I truly thought Noble would kill his father a few times. He'd punch so hard with those hobnailed hands of his that blood would spurt out of my grandfather's nose, and sometimes, he'd come up spitting out a tooth.

The violence was bad, but his words were so much worse. More than once, I was the slowest of the bunch, and he'd grab me by my belt loop and shake me, shouting in my face, drops of spittle smelling like whiskey spraying all over me. "The biggest mistake I ever made," he'd growl, "Was not to have

killed every one of you little bastards when you were born."
Sometimes, in those frightening moments, I wished he had.

But I knew he couldn't really hurt me. I had my beloved
Sylvania's protection.

You never knew when Daddy was going to get mad. It
wasn't any one thing or another that set him off. He always
had a gun on his hip, and that meant he was always scary, even
when he thought he was being funny. I saw him sit on the sofa,
asking Charlie to bet him if he could shoot the legs off the
kitchen table from where he sat. Bam. Bam bam bam. Four
shots. Four more bullets in the kitchen wall. Four legs still on
the kitchen table.

Charlie laughed when Daddy missed, and Daddy swung
that gun toward Charlie. "You think it's funny?"

"No, sir," Charlie said, swallowing his laugh and nearly
choking on it. Charlie was as tall as Daddy by then, but Daddy
had about a hundred pounds on Charlie. Charlie was all arm
bones and leg bones as a teenager. Daddy had the meaty arms
of someone who'd lifted stone blocks all day. Charlie didn't do
that well in school, but he was plenty smart enough to know
not to get under Daddy's skin.

"I'd like to see you hit your mark from this distance."

"I can't."

"That's right, you can't." Daddy kept the gun trained on Charlie for a few more beats, like he was trying to decide if he was satisfied, then shoved it back in his belt where it lived.

One day, I came home from school and saw my Daddy passed out on the couch, his hand twitching around that gun on his lap as he snored. Things were peaceful when Daddy slept, but you never knew what would wake him, so I took no chances. I went to my Holy of Holies.

Only it wasn't dark anymore. Daddy had shot three holes in the staircase wall, allowing three rays of light to stream through. It was so dark under the staircase that any light coming in from the outside burned like rays of sunshine. I wanted to be sad about losing my darkness, but the dust swirling in the beams caught my attention. It was a kaleidoscope of activity, and I was fascinated by it. I imagined the dust particles as tiny beings sent by my beloved Sylvania to watch over me as I sheltered from the battlefield that existed all around me.

Those three beams of light were a reminder that nothing was entirely safe from the battle.

I'm an old man now with chronic hip pain. Until I get to the hospital for a replacement, it's a constant struggle to keep a smile on my face while I hurt so much. Lucky for me, I never lost access to that secret place where my beloved Sylvania could keep me safe. I can close my eyes and disassociate, returning to snuggling into that loving, warm female presence.

Once, when I was a very small child, we were visiting Sylvania, and a family of nine came to visit. Sylvania only had a one-bedroom cottage. Finding a spot to sleep was hard, so I just didn't. Sylvania saw me walking around crying late at night, and she asked, "Baby, what's wrong?"

"I got no place to sleep."

"Get on up in here with your granny." I hopped up into her old metal frame bed, the springs squeaking so loudly I thought I would wake everyone in the house. She smelt so good, like dried apples. As soon as I had that thought, I heard my tummy rumble. She held me tight and said, "Someday you are gonna be old just like me, and I want you to remember this moment and feel how much your Granny loves you." I'm an old man now, and I can remember that moment, and I still feel how much she loves me.

Granny has been gone from this Earth for decades, but that doesn't mean she's all the way gone. She used her empathy to take the measure of my energy when she was alive, and she had such a precise bead on it that even now, from the great beyond, she can find my frequency and make the harmonics dance.

A few years ago, before my doctor would schedule surgery for my hip, I had to go to physical therapy. Part of the PT was massage therapy. I'd had massages before, and while they always felt good, I didn't have a lot of hope that it would do anything for the skeletal, deep pain I felt. I lay on the table, face down, and went to the place I always went to, the place with the music, the colors, and the presence of my beloved Sylvania. I shut off my active thoughts, as I always did, and simply experienced the warmth and safety of my Holy place.

Suddenly, I felt another presence there. For the first time in sixty years, someone besides my grandmother had joined me. I stiffened with fright, then relaxed as I realized it was the massage therapist. In order to do his job, he used his hands to tap into my energy and found the same vibrations that my beloved Sylvania had found.

When the hour was over, as I dressed behind a screen, I asked him if he had felt what I did.

"I didn't know how to explain it," he said.

Of course, he didn't. He'd simply tried to connect with my energy frequency to serve me better, not expecting a nuclear reactor's worth of energy.

To this day, I believe that my beloved Sylvania recognized the massage therapist's talents and orchestrated the whole thing.

Chapter Three

Mama didn't have a driver's license, but even if she did, it wouldn't have mattered. She didn't have a car to drive. Even if she'd had a car, it likely wouldn't have been large enough for her and her seven children.

We walked wherever we went. If we were going to the store or church, we walked. We should have walked to the government offices for food stamps, but Daddy was a proud man and would rather see us starve to death than have him look bad. We all walked together wherever we went. I'd like to say we walked in a row, Charlie at the head and me at the caboose, all lined up in size order like a parade of ducklings. But we weren't that regulated. We moved in a mob, circling like a school of fish, on high alert for predators.

Predators could be anywhere. We weren't afraid of child snatchers or wild animals. There was too much safety in our numbers for that. Instead, we were wary of regular people, of the other children at school who would taunt us for our shabby clothes and lack of transportation, and of the adults who would judge Mama for having more kids than she could handle. We weren't above throwing a punch or whipping tail if need be.

More often than not, though, it was the kids who were cruel. Adults, especially women, seemed drawn to me. I had silver-blonde hair. My beloved Sylvania called it Fairy Hair because it was too fine and gleaming to have come from this world. My Uncle Lowell nicknamed me "Jack Frost" because only a character from a fairy story could look like I did.

We must have appeared a menacing group when we were out and about, seven scrappy-looking kids and our hard-worn Mama. I was likely the most approachable, being the smallest. Between my size and my glittering hair, adults, especially women, would often approach me and comment on it. About half of them were bold enough to stroke my hair, all the while asking Mama where on Earth I'd gotten it as if a woman as poor and desperate as Mama couldn't possibly have given birth to something so precious without some kind of intervention.

"He's born with it. That's all I can say," Mama would reply. She'd yank me away from these fawning ladies. All of Mama's children were beautiful, but I was the baby and the only one with that hair, and she didn't want strangers touching her treasure.

I'm not sure where it came from. Mama's hair was brown, and Daddy didn't have much at all. What he did looked like he'd been left out in the rain, and it had started to rust. The older I got, the more I believed it was one more thing I received when Sylvania had placed her magic hedge of protection around me.

* * *

I had a big imagination and used it when walking around the woods near my house. Like I said, it was awfully easy to slip away and get lost for hours at a time. There were so many kids to keep track of, so much noise and chaos, that it would be a long while before anyone missed me.

I never got in trouble. I wasn't the kind of child who spent his time in the woods shooting squirrels with a slingshot or climbing trees to fall out of. Instead, I wandered around the woods because it was peaceful there, and I could think my own thoughts without the noise of my brothers and sisters crowding in.

We didn't have a television, but our neighbors did, and they'd invited us over to watch *The Wizard of Oz.* I was too young to comprehend the lessons Dorothy learned at the end. All I knew was I wanted to hide in Dorothy's basket with Toto and run away with her. I clapped when Dorothy found herself in the magical, colorful land of Oz. Our little house in the Miami Valley of Ohio felt like Kansas to me. I wanted to find adventure, friendship, and meaning the way Dorothy had in Oz. I'd wander around the woods, expecting to find the Tin Man rusted and still behind the trees or the Cowardly Lion hiding from me because he was afraid.

Years later, maybe decades, I realized the folly in what I tried to do. I looked for magic behind the trees without realizing that the trees themselves were magic. The towering oak trees had been there for one hundred years or more, bearing witness to history and keeping its secrets. There was an amazing life that surrounded me. I didn't need to go to Emerald City to find it. If only I'd known then that I had every right to be here. I had value, and I was worthy was a child of the universe with a purpose and a mission. Not even poverty or a battlefield could keep me from accomplishing what I was meant to do.

I think Mama did know it then. That was how she made it through. She didn't dream of fame or fortune or ruby slippers.

Her goal was survival. She wanted to keep us all alive. At the end of the day, if we were all together under one roof, it was a successful day. If she had more than three ingredients at a time to make dinner, it was a great day. They weren't all great days, but they were mostly successful, and that's more than most people get.

I admire Mama for that. She led by example, but I wish she'd taught us those lessons earlier and with more vehemence. I understand wanting to leave a legacy and having your imprint on the world last longer than your body, but ambition leads to disappointment. Wanting more makes you think what you have isn't enough, and then you miss the magic in a cricket's song.

We could all use a little more magic. My beloved Sylvania was shot through with magic, and that's what made her so special.

Chapter Four

My parents lived in many different houses, toting along an ever-growing number of children. By the time I came around, however, they had started to settle into one place. I remember going to that house for the first time, though I couldn't have been more than two or three.

A wooden sidewalk led up to a pale green house. My mother was carrying me, and I buried my face in her itchy coat to keep warm. I hated that coat, though Mama always wore it as soon as there was a chill in the air. It was gray and black plaid with wide lapels and large wooden buttons, the same color as the wooden sidewalk. One of the buttons was missing, and one of the boards in the sidewalk was missing, although Mama didn't see it because I was squirming in her arms against the itchy coat. Her foot went through the hole in the sidewalk, and we teetered and toppled but never fell. It doesn't seem like she could have kept her balance without twisting her ankle, but she did. It cemented my knowledge that no matter what, Mama would keep me upright and safe as long as I was in her arms. My beloved Sylvania's hedge of protection would see to it.

That house at 407 Forest Street was in the middle of what felt like a forest to me. There were trees everywhere, and you could not see your neighbors. I know now how primitive it was, but at the time, we were primitive people and it didn't bother us any to go tromping across the yard to the outhouse when we needed to do our business.

Nowadays, you'd say that house had potential. That's where it stayed, though, in the land of what could have been. My daddy had all the skills he needed to fix up that house and make it luxurious, but he didn't. He didn't seem to mind seeing us pump water from the well, and when the well went dry, we took what we needed from a pool hall that was through the woods behind our house. They had a spigot outside, and no one seemed to notice the passel of dirty kids with buckets. Or maybe they noticed and just felt sorry enough for us not to say anything.

Eventually, the city got word of the conditions in our house and condemned it, but no one told Noble Keeton where he could and couldn't live. That house wasn't much, but it did keep us from freezing to death in the winter and dry from the summer rains, which was enough for us.

When Daddy was in a working mood, he'd lay bricks with his friend Hank. Hank had a pretty wife named Tammy. I remember meeting Tammy for the first time. Daddy had somehow managed to buy a brand new car, a Chevelle. He took me out for a Saturday drive. My brothers and sisters were mad that Daddy took me. They were older, and they thought they should have the privilege. Daddy never took me anywhere, and it felt better than Christmas to me. I didn't care that I'd have frogs in my pockets or one of the girls would tell Mama I hit her just to get me in trouble. I got to ride with Daddy, and that was payment enough for their payback.

I was about five at the time, but even then, I knew he was drunk. I can't imagine why Mama let me go off with him, but I suppose when you have that many children, and you fear the fist of the man you live with, you have to choose your battles.

We left the house. I sat on my knees on the passenger seat, my head out the window so I wouldn't miss anything. We drove past our house and through town and out on a one-lane bridge. The bridge had no guardrails, just a steel rope marking the edge. I pulled my head in the window when Daddy swiped that steel rope the first time.

Not long past the bridge, we stopped at a little house with peeling white paint. I don't guess it was a fancy house, now that I know what fancy houses really look like, but compared to our little shack, it felt like a mansion to me. We walked up the clean-swept porch and Daddy knocked on the door.

A lady opened the door and said, "Hey, Noble. What can I do for ya?"

The lady wore makeup and had her hair fixed just so. She looked like Priscilla Presley to me.

"Is Hank around?"

The lady's smile was so bright and warm it could melt butter. "Why, no, Noble. He ain't. He went fishing, and he won't be home 'til after dark. Why don't you and this handsome little fella come in for a spell." She looked down at me, and I was afraid my knees would buckle. She brought us to her living room. "You want a Co-cola, little man?"

It took me a moment to realize she was talking to me. "Yes, Ma'am." This was my lucky day. A ride in Daddy's car *and* a Co-cola. Usually, I just drank water from the buckets we hauled from the pool hall. A Co-cola was a real treat.

The lady went into the kitchen and came back with a small glass of something brown for Daddy and a whole bottle of Co-cola me. She handed it to me. I wanted to drink the whole thing down at once, but I knew it was something to be savored. I poured some into my mouth and held it there, the bubbles tickling my throat and the sugar seeping directly into my blood from underneath my tongue. Daddy and the lady started talking. I didn't listen to them. It seemed like boring grownup talk to me.

Eventually, I slid off the chair I was sitting on and picked up a colorful magazine off her table. Daddy saw me doing it and snapped, "Jackie Lynn. Don't you touch Miz Tammy's things."

I dropped the magazine.

Miz Tammy laughed a tinkling laugh and slapped Daddy's chest. I expected him to get mad at her and maybe hit her back like he'd do with Mama, but he just smiled at her. "Noble, let the boy look. It's just *National Geographic*. He might learn something."

Miz Tammy took a few steps over to me and bent down to pick up the magazine. She handed it back to me. "You look all you want, honey. Keep yourself busy with it. I need to show your Daddy something in the back."

She took my Daddy by the hand and led him into a bedroom. She shut the door, and I heard the lock click as it closed. Miz Tammy and Daddy started making noises in there. I might have only been five years old, but I knew what those noises were. When you lived in a house as small as ours, no one had any secrets. As I drank my Co-cola, I thought, *this must be one of those whorehouses Mama talks about.* I wasn't judging; just trying to make sense of where I was.

I closed my eyes, wishing for all the world that I could go to my Holy of Holies, the place under the stairs. I didn't want to be here, listening to Miz Tammy and Daddy making those noises. I wanted to hear the celestial symphonies in my sanctuary, get lost in the darkness, and feel the presence of my beloved Sylvania and God.

But my Holy of Holies didn't exist at Miz Tammy's house, and I wasn't yet good enough to get there from wherever I was, so I sat back down in the chair and took another sip of Co-cola. I couldn't read, but I did like the pictures in *National Geographic*. My brothers and I played cowboys and Indians all the time, using sticks as guns and bigger branches as horses. That magazine had lots of pictures of the Old West, some photographs, some illustrations, all wonderful. I dove headfirst into them, listening to the shouts, clip-clopping of the horses' hooves, and the out-of-tune piano playing coming from a saloon, letting it all drown out the noises coming from Miz Tammy's room.

I don't know how much time had passed when Miz Tammy and Daddy came back out. Miz Tammy ruffled my hair and said, "You are a good boy, ain'tcha? Do you like that magazine? You can take it with you if you want." Daddy narrowed his eyes like there was something bad behind her offer, but since he couldn't figure it out, he let me take it.

We piled back into Daddy's car. "I'll see you soon," Miz Tammy said, kissing Daddy on the cheek. I saw Miz Tammy get into her car. She took off in the other direction.

We weren't home for twenty minutes, and my older brother had already torn the cover of my *National Geographic* trying to snatch it away from me when we heard a car pull up outside. We never heard cars in our driveway, so we all stopped what we were doing and ran to the door.

It was Miz Tammy. She was holding some flat boxes and wore a great big, toothy smile. "Well, hello, Jackie Lynn. Hello boys, hello girls. I brought pizza."

Pizza? I'd never had pizza before. Pizza was as exotic to me as monkey brains might have been. I started bouncing on the balls of my feet, reaching for the boxes.

Mama looked at Miz Tammy. I guess they'd met before because she said, "Tammy," and nodded. Tammy nodded back and said, "Virginia."

"Thanks for bringing us supper. That was right kind of you." Mama's words were nice, but the way she said them made them sound like she was cursing.

Miz Tammy's smile stayed on her face like it was painted there. "Oh, well, Hank is out fishing and I find myself getting lonely sometimes. You're doing me a favor by keeping me company."

Miz Tammy put the boxes down in the kitchen, and we swarmed around her, opening them up and pulling out pieces for ourselves.

By the end of the evening, Daddy was sitting in his spot on the sofa, passed out drunk, and Mama and Miz Tammy had their heads together, talking so fast it sounded like chirping birds to me. Somehow, they got to be friends, though you wouldn't think they'd be. Maybe Mama was glad that Miz Tammy had taken a burden off her.

Not long after that, Miz Tammy and Hank moved into a house down the street from us. I think Daddy spent as much time at their house as he did at ours. Miz Tammy and Mama kept on being friends, and Miz Tammy was the one who finally taught Mama how to drive a car.

Chapter Five

Noble had a cousin named Randall Hutchinson. He was one of many preachers in our little corner of Kentucky. Daddy didn't much like Randall. I guess because he was everything that Daddy wasn't.

Mama would try to take us to church, but Daddy would accuse her of wanting to be with Cousin Randall. I wasn't old enough to have my own opinions about Cousin Randall, but I knew Grandma Ruby adored him. And he was kind to my family and me, even with Daddy's venom.

Randall would walk the gravel roads of Wright View. Wright View was the actual name of our neighborhood, though Daddy called it Wrong View because we were clearly on the wrong side of the tracks. Randall always dressed impeccably, and his shoes always had a shine, even with all the gravel dust that should have clung to him. Randall was untouchable like that. I think that's why Daddy didn't like him.

One day, he told Mama they would be having a revival the coming week. "I hope you'll make it, Virginia, and bring your young 'uns." "I'll try," she said, but she didn't make it. I think Mama knew we weren't all going to make it when she said we'd try.

Grandma Ruby, on the other hand, would not be missing one night of a revival preached by her favorite nephew. My cousin Carolyn would be visiting Grandma Ruby because Carolyn's baby sister was in the hospital. Grandma Ruby invited me to come along to keep Carolyn company. Daddy didn't argue about me going – I don't think he cared much where I went, only where Mama went.

That night, as the service came to a close, while my cousin Sandy played the piano as her daddy, Randall, gave an altar call, the spirit of the Lord caught him heavy. I can close my eyes and be there, hearing Randall's great big booming voice spreading over the tent, all heads bowed. "If you are troubled and heavy laden and would like to remove all your burdens, bring them here. Leave them at Jesus' feet." Randall spread his arms wide, inviting the congregation to come join him.

I was troubled and heavy laden, as young as I was. Randall's words gave me a hope I don't think I'd ever felt. I wanted to meet this man Jesus. If he wanted to help me, I would accept his offer. Daddy was too proud to accept help, but I wasn't. I stood up and marched to the front of the tent, head bowed in front of Randall. That night, I gave my life to a man named Jesus. I have never regretted it.

* * *

I was seven, and it was Christmastime, though you wouldn't know it from our house. There weren't any baking smells because Mama had no ingredients to bake with. There weren't any presents piled up in a corner or under a tree because there wasn't a tree or money to buy gifts with. I know it made Mama sad that there weren't any pies or presents. She told us that Santa couldn't find us in this corner of Ohio. We all knew by then that Santa wasn't real, and if he was real, he wasn't worth believing in, so this was nothing new.

Mama begged Daddy to get us a tree. "We live in the woods, Noble. If you can't provide a real Christmas for your family, the least you could do is cut down a tree."

"What do we need a tree for?" Daddy snapped back. "We ain't got nothing to decorate it with. It's just going to sit in a corner and die."

Mama didn't cry often, but she cried then. "I just want a little piece of holiday in here."

She aggravated Daddy so much that he left and didn't come back. Christmas Eve came and went. On Christmas morning, we could see Daddy's truck parked outside Miz Tammy's house and what appeared to be the bottom half of a twenty-foot blue spruce. We were later told Daddy had cut it right out of a man's front yard. It was just the beginning of what seemed to be an obsession with Miz Tammy.

Since Daddy wasn't around, we took what decorations we had and strung them up all over our living room and played our one Andy Williams album on a turntable my brother had found at the dump and fixed up. It wasn't a fancy Christmas, but it was a nice one with my brothers and sisters and Mama and a peaceful one without Daddy around.

Of course, Daddy didn't stay away forever. Daddy came home just as some ladies from Cousin Randall's church dropped by with some food and gifts. We were all happy to have the food cooked lovingly by those sweet Baptist women and to have any kind of gifts at all.

Daddy, on the other hand, looked like he might kill someone. "Get this out of my house. We don't need any of your Christian charity." He said 'Christian' like it was something to be ashamed of. I think he just about scared those poor ladies to death.

I remember feeling humiliated and sad for those kind women. "No good deed goes unpunished," I heard one of the ladies say.

"Not a thing in that house for that family to eat," her friend replied. "You would have thought that fool was a Kennedy or Rockefeller the way he carried on about not needing anything."

Chapter Six

Noble received word that his father, Clent, had died. He didn't much like his father, but obligations were obligations, and he would need to go to Kentucky for the funeral. Though Noble's dislike of folks wasn't always rational, he hit the nail on the head this time. Clent was a dreadful man. I'm sure, but compared to his own raising, Noble probably felt like the father of the year.

In addition to being mean and ornery, Clent was a child predator. He had taken an interest in my 14-year-old cousin, Jeanette. Jeanette was a pretty girl, but she was also a little strange—probably because of what Clent did, though I'll never know for sure. She had a habit of sucking on a lock of her hair, and her beautiful blue eyes were hard as marble. She hardly ever smiled. I can't tell you if Jeanette had a taste for murder or if Clent's abuse drove her to it, but either way, she saw a perfect opportunity to quench her thirst and exact her revenge.

She wasn't very shy about telling us how she did it. First, she got him drunk. That was the easy part since Clent was drunk most of the time. When he wasn't, it was because he couldn't afford the liquor to do it. He started hollering at Jeanette to get him another glass of that whiskey she had bought him, and she said sweet as pie that she would. What she brought him looked like whiskey, but it was really a glass of turpentine.

It took two days for the poison to take effect. By all reports, it was a terrible and painful way to die. But the murder was complete, and despite the number of people in the family who knew what had happened, no one complained.

In those days, because of his age and the nature of his death, the coroner wanted an autopsy. Clent's reputation was widespread in those parts, and they ruled it an accident. Foul play was suspected, but my family wasn't in the mood to kick up a fuss about anyone being held accountable. Most of the family didn't care if someone killed him. Those who really knew him had reason to celebrate; they slept easier knowing he would never hurt another child.

About the same time, Miz Tammy told Mama she was hell-bent on getting out of this Podunk town. A young singer named Glen Campbell had written a song about Galveston, Texas, and from that song, she decided it was everything she ever wanted. She knew better than to ask Hank directly, so she talked Noble into convincing Hank they needed to move and get out of the cold winters of Ohio. She told Mama that it didn't take a lot of convincing. Hank brought the idea up to her, and she put Glen Campbell on the record player. He was sold.

Of course, Noble wasn't letting Miz Tammy go across the country without him. Under the guise of helping them move, off to Texas went Noble and the love of his life and her husband. As far as I know, he felt nothing but glee leaving Virginia and her seven burdens behind.

Without Noble to tell her no, Virginia immediately signed up for all the public assistance we could get. Those books of food stamp coupons felt like we hit the big time. As the kids would say today, we were ballin'. Mama wasn't shy at all about buying milk, cheese, eggs, and meat with those food stamps, even when I heard several people say she better hope Noble Keeton doesn't find out. Everyone knew that if Noble knew Mama was taking government assistance, he would come back to Ohio just to kick her ass and burn her food stamps.

Hank and Tammy settled into their house, and Noble moved into an efficiency motel. They had been there a month or so, and Noble had no plans to leave. Why should he? He had his plate of cake and was eating it, too.

Mama thought the story was funny, how it ended up, so she'd tell it again and again as we got older. Hank was Noble's drinking and card buddy; Tammy was a nymphomaniac. Noble and Hank would work all week and party all weekend. For a little while, everything seemed right in the world of Noble and Hank. Until it wasn't.

Noble arrived at the Conley house one Sunday morning at about 11 o'clock. All three of them had spent Saturday night out listening to local country-western bands. Just as Noble got there, Miz Tammy pulled into the driveway. She'd gone to the store and come back with all the ingredients for a good time.

Noble and Miz Tammy went into the house, anticipating a great morning. Hank was passed out on the couch. Noble called Hank's name a few times to see if he was sleeping or truly unconscious, and he didn't respond. Tammy said, "Hank, git up." When he didn't stir, she said, a little bit louder, "Hank. Noble's here. Git up off that couch."

Noble picked up an empty Jack Daniels bottle on the coffee table. Laughing, he said, "He musta drunk this whole bottle to be this dead." He slapped Miz Tammy on her backside.

Miz Tammy giggled. "Noble! What if he wakes up?"

"With that much Jack in him, we'll be lucky if he wakes up today." Noble placed a hand on her breast and nuzzled her neck.

"Noble! I can't do this with Hank right there."

Nothing deterred Noble when he had an idea in his head. "So let's go somewhere he ain't."

They moved into the bedroom and, according to what he told Mama later, Hank gave them twenty minutes to get into what they were going to get up to. Turns out, he'd taken an empty bottle out of the trash and pretended to be passed out, but he was stone cold sober. He'd begun to suspect that Noble hadn't come to Texas to spend time with his buddy Hank so much as to spend time with Tammy, and he wanted to see for himself.

Hank got off the couch and tiptoed to the bedroom door. He threw it open and saw with his own eyes everything he needed to know. He wasn't really that upset with Tammy; he knew not to expect any better out of her. But Noble was his best friend, and he had betrayed him.

Instead of confronting them then and there, he walked into the kitchen and pulled out one of the new bottles of Jack Tammy had just bought and began to empty it into his throat. Noble and Tammy came running, half-dressed, to follow him, looking sheepish. Hank started to move about like a bear waking from a long winter's nap. "What are you two up to?"

Tammy, apparently seizing the opportunity he'd given her, pretended that her husband hadn't just caught her and Noble doing things they oughtn't have been doing. "We are doing all the things you ought to be doing, you lazy bum." She laughed playfully.

Noble and Tammy waited a beat to see how Hank was going to react. When he didn't, the day went off as planned. They drank and smoked and played cards and laughed the way they usually did.

As Noble was getting ready to leave later that evening, Hank said, "I'm going to drive tomorrow."

"Okay.

Hank said, "I'll be around about 6:30. Don't you be late. I'm not losing any more work because you can't get your sorry ass ready in time."

"Damn, Hank. I'll be ready."

The next morning, Hank arrived at Noble's motel at 5 AM. He carried a steel pipe. Noble's door was unlocked. Hank turned the knob slowly so it wouldn't make any noise and padded across the brown shag carpet. Noble was lying on his stomach, dead to the world. With everything he had in him, Hank got one good blow to Noble's head and went back to his car, heading to work.

Hank told everyone at work he thought Noble had gone back to Ohio, and that's why he hadn't shown up. When he got home, Hank gave Tammy a hug and a kiss and, with a smile on his face, told his sweet wife, "I killed your lover. If you open your mouth and tell anyone, you'll be going to jail with me."

After three days and some complaints from neighboring guests, the hotel attendant went to Noble's room. He found Noble lying face down in a pool of dried blood. The man thought he was dead. Instead of the police, he called the coroner. The coroner examined Noble, probably expecting him to be one more shiftless victim of a dangerous lifestyle and cried out when he discovered a faint pulse. "This man is still alive!" He reached over to the phone on the nightstand and called an ambulance.

Galveston was a big enough city that it took a while to get the ambulance to the hotel room. Still, the stubborn mule that he was, Noble had hung on for three days. Surely a few more minutes wasn't going to make a difference. The paramedics loaded him in the ambulance as the police swarmed the room.

The police, making a lot of the same assumptions the coroner had, didn't investigate all that fully. They noted Noble's place on the bed and where the entry and exit wounds were in a bare-bones report. Since they couldn't find his wallet or any money, they determined it was an obvious robbery and closed the case, not wasting any effort in finding Noble's attacker.

No one pushed them to, either. Just like his father, no one really had hard feelings toward anyone who gave Noble his due.

Ten days later, Noble woke up in a hospital in Houston. Mama and all of Noble's siblings had made the dutiful trek across the country and were standing around his bed.

"Where the hell am I?" Those were the first words he'd spoken in all that time.

"You're in the hospital in Houston," Mama told him.

"What the hell happened?"

Mama hadn't yet heard the whole story, so she told him she didn't know. She could, however, tell her what the doctors had told her. One-third of his skull was missing, and they'd had to put a metal plate in his head to protect what was left of his brains.

Eventually, he was stabilized, and the folks at the hospital sat down with Mama. "He's going to need a calm place to recover."

Mama laughed. Calm could be found almost anywhere, but not any place where Noble was. Still, she promised to do what she could and loaded Noble in his car to begin the long drive back to Ohio.

Mama sent a letter home, where my brother Charlie, now an older teenager who had dropped out of school to work, was taking care of the rest of us. Charlie received word of what was going on and, as always, set to work. He managed to find an old farmhouse out in the middle of nowhere and rented it with his income that was steadier than any Noble had managed to bring in for us.

We lived in that farmhouse for the next year. Life wasn't any easier for us in the farmhouse, mainly because Noble's usual temper was made worse by the constant headaches he endured. He was sober, too, maybe for the first time since he was a teenager. Mama wouldn't bring him any alcohol or use any of the precious money Charlie brought in for that poison. Noble was too injured to make too loud of a fuss or get up and get it on his own, but he could still cuss a blue streak while lying there in his bed.

The farmhouse was the prettiest house we'd ever lived in, but it wasn't in such great repair, having been empty for a good long while before we moved in. The critters that had taken up residence in the absence of people were none too interested in sharing their shelter. I was used to finding mice and spiders in whatever house we lived in, but these creatures were bold. I hated feeling the rats running across the top of the covers as I tried to sleep. Even now, just thinking about it makes my skin crawl.

It seemed like forever before we knew whether Noble would recover into his old self. We weren't sure we wanted him to, either. He wasn't pleasant as an invalid, but he couldn't hurt us. We knew Noble was getting better when he started getting meaner and nastier. I don't know which was worse: sober and nasty Noble or drunk and mean Noble. My brothers and sisters and I spent long hours debating the question, not that we could choose for him. But we whiled away many hours arguing the pluses and minuses of each.

Despite his limitations, it turned out Noble was the brains behind the Texas venture. Without Noble's wiliness, Galveston lost its charm. Despite nearly killing his friend, Hank found work without Noble uninteresting, and Miz Tammy was bored without someone to dally with. It wasn't long before Hank and Miz Tammy returned from the Texas shores to the gray skies of Ohio. The first stop they made when they rolled into town was at our doorstep. They'd heard that

Daddy had no memory of who had hurt him, and they said they came round to see about their old friend.

"Oh, Noble," Miz Tammy cooed. Noble hadn't gotten up off the recliner when they came in. Miz Tammy made him act like a helpless child. I guess he figured that was the best way to get her to touch him without Hank knowing why. "They never did find the robbers that had done this terrible thing to our best and dearest friend."

"Police are useless," Noble growled. "You gots to do these things yourself." He nodded his chin at Hank. "You ever gone looking yourself?"

"I did," said Hank. "But it ain't like anyone did this to you cuz they was mad at you. They just wanted your money. Hard to track that kind of guy."

Noble grunted, squinching up his face as Miz Tammy bent down to kiss his head. Mama said later that Tammy figured that if Hank knew she'd played her part, she could indulge in a little affection.

It turned out the only medicine Noble Keeton needed to regain his will to live was the smell of Miz Tammy's Chanel

No. 5. She always joked that, just like Marilyn, it was the only thing she ever wore to bed.

As soon as Hank and Mis Tammy left, Noble returned to his old self, mean as ever. We had to readjust our evaluation; it wasn't drunk Noble or sober Noble that was the meanest – lonely Noble was the orneriest version of all. We were all about to see just how mean he could get. His temper might have been back, but he was still ailing and couldn't get too far on his own. So he was stuck at home for a long while, getting irritated with us kids and resenting Mama for not being Miz Tammy.

Chapter Seven

Summer of 1970 came on hot that year. On my first day back in little Kentucky, I was lucky enough to find an empty sofa to sleep on. Outside, I could hear dogs barking and the call of birds and a radio playing *American Woman*. I woke up that first morning, my cheek pebbled with marks from the rough fabric on the sofa, sweaty and sticky. It was way too hot to stay inside.

I found a stale piece of bread that would serve as my breakfast and went outside to explore my new neighborhood. Right away, I saw a girl who looked about my age. She was drawing a hopscotch board in the middle of our dead-end road. Before I even asked, she told me her name was Ann Marie, and we played hopscotch for a while until a lady came out of the door of the house nearest to us. "Ann Marie!" She called. "Time for you to get your breakfast."

"I got to go," Ann Marie told me.

"Okay. 'Sgood to meet you," I mumbled, trying to remember my manners.

"Who's your new friend?" The lady called over to Ann Marie.

"That there's Jackie Lynn. He just moved in up the street.

"Jackie Lynn! You eat breakfast yet?"

I stopped in my tracks and turned. "No'm."

"You want to eat with Ann Marie? We don't have anything fancy, just eggs and bacon and some store-bought biscuits."

Eggs? Bacon? Biscuits? All at the same meal? I fairly ran into Ann Marie's yard. "That would be great, ma'am."

Ann Marie's mama told me to call her Mrs. Bentley, and I did. She fed me a heap of eggs and some bacon, and when I'd gobbled it all up, she asked me if I wanted any more.

As soon as Ann Marie finished eating, she scampered off like a stray cat. I was still working on my third biscuit and finished it before standing up. "Thanks for breakfast, Mrs. Bentley. It was real good."

Mrs. Bentley stood up and took my plate from me, placing it in the sink. "Any time, Jackie Lynn." She looked at the pile of dishes in the sink.

"May I do those for ya? It's the least I can do." I was so grateful for the ache in my full belly that I'd have scrubbed her whole house for her if she wanted me to.

"That would really help me out." I could hear the appreciation in her voice, something I wasn't used to hearing from adults. "I guess I'd better finish my gardening before the sun gets too high and burns me out of the yard."

I finished up the dishes, dried and stacked them all nicely, and hung the dish towel nice and neat in hopes she might ask me back. Mrs. Bentley seemed like the nicest lady I'd ever met. So I went outside and found her kneeling in the yard. "Do you need any help?"

Mrs. Bentley cocked her head. "You want to help me in the garden?"

"Yes, ma'am. My Aunt Wanda has a garden, and we don't go to her house much, but when we do, I like helping her."

"Doesn't your Mama need your help with something?"

I hung my head. "No, ma'am. Mama's got a lot to do, but there's four of us still at home, and I'm the youngest. I think mostly she just thinks I get underfoot. My Daddy's not home most of the time.

Mrs. Bentley narrowed her eyes like she was trying to decide something. Finally, she nodded and said, "Do you have strong hands? If so, you can pull weeds."

I helped Mrs. Bentley all morning. I was there so long she fed me lunch, and then I helped her with chores inside the house all afternoon. She let me eat dinner with her and Ann Marie. Ann Marie had an older sister who came home right before dinner. She came sailing through the door and said, "Mama? Who's this boy in our house?"

Mrs. Bentley laughed. "Gail, this here is Jackie Lynn. He's new to the neighborhood."

Mr. Bentley came home soon after Gail, and Mrs. Bentley introduced me in the same way. Mr. Bentley wasn't as friendly as Mrs. Bentley. He shook my hand and politely said, "Pleased to meet you, Jackie Lynn," but he never smiled. I'm sure he was thinking *one more mouth to feed.*

Mr. Bentley turned from me and bent down to kiss Mrs. Bentley on the cheek, which immediately made me like him despite his stern demeanor. "Did you have a good day, Gertrude?" I fairly laughed, imagining Noble asking Mama if she'd had a good day.

"I certainly did. Jackie Lynn here was a huge help. He pulled all the weeds in the vegetable garden for me and did the dishes without being asked." She smiled a prideful smile at me, another thing I'd never received from an adult.

"Well then, Jackie Lynn," Mr. Bentley said. "I guess I'm glad we found you. Gertrude has a habit of feeding the strays that wander around here, but none of the cats she feeds do the dishes for her."

"Wash up, Jackie Lynn." Mrs. Bentley handed me a full-sized towel and a small washcloth. "If you're going to eat at my table, you're not going to do it that dirty. Get in there and take a shower."

I couldn't remember the last time I'd taken a shower. We only had a tub at our house, and no one reminded us to use it very often. I started to protest that I didn't want to hold off everyone's dinner to take a shower I didn't need, but Mrs.

Bentley cut me off. "I don't care how hungry you are. Cleanliness is next to Godliness."

We ate a dinner of meatloaf and big fat potatoes and carrots that had been cut into discs and cooked in butter. It might have been the fanciest dinner I ever remembered eating. As soon as I finished, I started to clear the table and went to do the dishes. Mrs. Bentley put a hand on my shoulder and said, "No, Jackie Lynn. It will be dark soon, and you've already helped enough today. Go home to your Mama. I don't want to be accused of kidnapping."

The next morning, as soon as I got up, I walked over to the Bentleys' house and knocked on the door to ask Mrs. Bentley if she needed help with anything. I think I spent more time at the Bentleys that summer than I did my own. No one really noticed that I was gone, but they did notice that I was putting on weight. We were all skinny, rangy kids, but Mrs. Bentley's generous cooking put some meat on my bones.

So, I lived with a borrowed name until I got out of high school. Years later, when I became an adult, a man, and tired of living my life on a name borrowed from my dead cousin, I took it upon myself to go to the courthouse and officially change my name to Jack Bentley Keeton—a man's name for a man, honoring the family that had nourished my body and my soul. I finally had an identity. I could then start living my own life and not the one my cousin never got to live.

The building we lived in had once been an old Air Force barrack. Sheriff Horner's daddy had bought some surplus metal barracks buildings from the Air Force after the war and had them moved to some old family land he had. He didn't do much to improve them besides connecting up the plumbing and electricity.

Because our house was an old military barrack, it wasn't set up like a regular house. It was long and skinny, and there were no doors on the rooms. It was barely a house, and never a home. When the Air Force owned it, there would have been bunk beds on either side of the structure. As it was, we only owned three beds. One went on one side for Mama and Daddy. On the other side were two beds, but it wasn't like they were for anyone in particular. They were for whoever got to them first. If you didn't get a bed, you'd dig into the assortment of worn blankets and pillows and make a pallet.

Every evening there was a scramble for bed space, the choicest pillows, and the softest blankets. As the youngest, I lost most of those fights, and after a while, I didn't fight at all.

I just made my bed on the scratchy sofa we'd gotten from Aunt Garnet, wearing socks to keep my feet warm and dissociating the best I could. There, in the dark, with the music of night birds and frogs, I could dive into the darkness, listening to the beautiful sounds of my Holy of Holies. I imagined the young airmen who stayed in this building. I could feel their fear absorbed into the metal walls. When they left the meager comfort of this barrack, they could not have known if they would survive. Their uncertainty resonated with me. In those days, I didn't know if I would survive, either. In some ways, I was jealous of those brave men. At least they had Air Force-issued clothing.

I never knew who had last worn the socks I was wearing. Of course, it wasn't like any of us owned much of anything. We didn't have our own dressers, much less our own drawers. Even if we did, Mama had too much going on to keep anything sorted. One drawer had socks and underwear in it, and we'd just find something that fit—or fit close enough—and wear it. I don't think we had a toothbrush between us. When our breath got foul, we'd rinse our mouths with baking soda and water or maybe wipe off our teeth with an old rag.

I didn't know that how we lived wasn't normal. I thought the Bentleys were the exception, not us. The Bentleys seemed rich to me, and it seemed foolish to compare our circumstances to theirs. I know now that Mr. Bentley was a factory worker, and they were what you'd call middle class, maybe even lower middle class.

That summer quickly came to an end. By this point, the Bentley family was figuring me out. Like Noble, I was very prideful and wasn't going to take anything I didn't earn. Unlike Noble, I was willing to work and unwilling to do without. School was about to start. It was clear to anyone with eyes that my wardrobe was lacking. My pants were too short and worn thin in places. I had been cutting cardboard to slide into my shoes to protect the bottom of my feet from the sharp ground I could feel through the holes in the soles. The cardboard did a pretty good job until it rained.

One day, Mama Bentley sat me down with a Sears and Roebuck catalog. "You, young man, have worked very hard this summer, and you have earned yourself some new clothes." The tone of her voice made it clear she would brook no argument.

I started to argue anyway, but I looked at her stern expression and noted that she'd used the word "earn." Maybe in her mind, it might have been charity, but she knew me well enough to know I wouldn't take it if it had been offered that way. "Thank you, ma'am," I said. And I began to look through the catalog.

I'd seen the Sears and Roebuck catalog before. Of course, I had. They came to everyone's mailbox. But I'd never looked at it before thinking I could actually have anything in it. Since I'd been born, I'd never worn a new piece of clothing. Being the youngest, I only wore clothes my brothers had already broken in.

I looked through it again and again. There were plaid wool coats that looked so much warmer than anything I'd ever owned. Striped knit shirts. Hooded sweatshirts. T-shirts in strong, vivid colors. Denim pants were so solid a blue I wondered if they'd feel like the faded, splotchy pair I had on or if they'd be something else entirely. Finally, after hours of pouring through page after page, I picked out a pair of jeans, a long-sleeved shirt, and a sweater.

"Jackie Lynn," Mrs. Bentley scolded.

I hung my head. The last thing I wanted to do was make Mrs. Bentley mad. "I'm sorry, ma'am. I picked out too much. I don't want to be a burden. I just got too excited."

Mrs. Bentley started to laugh, which made my shame burn hotter until she said, "Oh, sugar. I meant just the opposite. How much work do you think you've done this summer?"

"Dunno."

"Well. Let's do some math now." She took out a pad of paper and a pencil. "June has 30 days, and July has 31. That's about eight and a half weeks." You've been here almost every day, but let's say we take off that half-week. Eight times seven is fifty-six. So you've been here about fifty-six days. You with me so far?"

I nodded. "Every day you were here, you did chores for me. At least three hours, maybe more, but let's just say three hours." She made some scratches on the pad with her pencil. "Fifty-six days times three hours a day is one hundred sixty-eight hours you've worked."

That sure did sound like a lot of hours, but I couldn't argue with her math.

"Now," she continued. "Minimum wage is $1.65 an hour. If I'd had to pay you for those hours, that's what I would have paid you. One hundred sixty-eight times $1.65 is $277.20." She pushed the pad towards me. "Is my math right?"

I looked at what she'd written down, but I couldn't do math in my head. I knew Mrs. Bentley wouldn't lie, though, so I said, "Yes,m."

"So. You've got about thirty dollars' worth of clothes picked out. Does thirty dollars' worth of clothes for two hundred seventy-seven dollars' worth of work sound fair to you?"

I had no idea what to say. She couldn't possibly mean what I thought she meant. I gaped at her for a few moments before saying, "But you fed me a lot of meals, Mrs. Bentley."

"Jackie Lynn," she said, in a voice that brooked no argument. "It's math. You can't argue with numbers." I would start school with new clothes. I can remember each item the way most kids remember their first car. Mrs. Bentley bought me the first belt I ever owned. The first pair of socks I didn't have to share with my brothers. She was very good at guarding my dignity.

Chapter Eight

I had just turned 14. By my parents' standards, I was more or less a man, fully capable of working if I wanted to. I think if the law didn't say they had to provide for me, they probably would have shoved me out the door and told me to fend for myself.

It was late spring, and I had no curfew. I spent some nights at the Keeton house and some nights at the Bentley house. Mostly, it depended on what time I got home—the doors at the Bentley house locked at 9 o'clock. No one worried about me. All the adults just assumed that if I wasn't at one house, I was at the other.

One Friday night, I got rabble-rousing with my friends close to midnight. It was way too late even to try to get into the Bentleys' house. Virginia's doors were never locked. She worked nights, so she wasn't home yet and wouldn't be till probably two in the morning. I stripped down to my boxers and fell asleep on the sofa, hoping Mama would be quiet and not wake me when she came home.

I began to dream I was smothering. I couldn't catch my breath. I felt exposed and cold. With a stab of pain in my backside, I woke up. My face was being held down into my pillow by a strong hand. He'd pulled my boxers down and was trying to maneuver himself inside me.

I know I screamed. I must have screamed, but I heard nothing. The humiliation and pain hit me all at the same time, blinding me to everything. Being a Keeton, I knew how to fight, but being the youngest and smallest, I didn't know how to win. My thinking brain disappeared, and my 'fight or flight' reflex chose flight. I couldn't see my attacker or hear his voice, but I knew how much bigger he was than me. I couldn't challenge him and win, but I could get away.

I struggled to get him off me. The more I squirmed and kicked, the more he pushed, over and over, thrusting against me until he satisfied himself. Taking advantage of his brief dive into stolen ecstasy, I managed to roll out from underneath him. I grabbed my clothes from where I'd left them in a pile next to the couch and ran.

I knew there was an old car in the woods near my house that didn't run anymore. The kids in the neighborhood would sit in it and smoke and drink. It was dirty and ragged, but it looked like a sanctuary to me. I got in the backseat and slept. As soon as the sun came up, I went to the Bentleys' house. I jumped into the shower and stayed there for what felt like an hour, trying to scrub off the events of the previous evening.

I never did tell anyone what happened, not then. What would they do? I didn't think anyone would believe me, and if I'd admitted that a man had violated me that way, it would open me up to all kinds of ridicule.

I began to pull away from the Bentleys. I felt too soiled to be in their perfect home for long. I started hanging out at my cousin Sharon's house. More than anything else, I wanted to stay away from that dead-end street we lived on. I didn't know who the man was, but I knew he'd come back for me.

By mid-summer, I had been shot, and, in some way, that bullet wound saved me. After that, I didn't have to tell anybody I lived in constant danger; it was all over the local news.

Chapter Nine

Mama was down to three kids in the house, the oldest four having escaped as soon as they were old enough to get out. Daddy had left and moved into a trailer, or at least so he said. We knew he was staying most of the time with Miz Tammy.

I was all but living with the Bentley family. They took me everywhere. I went to church with them every Sunday and tagged along when they went to eat Chinese food for Sunday supper. On Tuesdays at the local steakhouse, they would introduce me as their son, and I prayed that it could somehow be true. Gail had blond hair, just like me. I think after a while, most people forgot I wasn't their natural-born son. I know I did.

I wasn't the only one who escaped. My sister Kathy stayed with her best friend Patty a lot. Linda did the best she could to stay away and keep away.

Mama never came looking for us. When she saw us, we were always cleaner than when she'd last seen us, and we appeared to be well-fed, so there was no reason for her to be concerned. Besides, she was busy. Mama had started corresponding with Hank just to drive Noble crazy.

I don't think Noble really cared. Mama knew Tammy wanted Hank out of the picture for good. By this time, Mama wanted her revenge on all of them, Tammy included, so she began telling Noble how Hank had been the one who nearly killed him. "It's true, Noble," I heard her say. "He told me next time he would finish the job."

Noble was never the kind of man to take a threat, even a third-party threat by someone who had an ax to grind, without reacting to it.

Hank and Tammy had a couple of kids at this point, even though they weren't living together anymore. Hank saw his kids on the weekends.

When Tammy and Noble were away from Tammy's kids, Tammy would start planting seeds. "Noble, the kids are telling me that Hank is unhappy that he didn't finish what he started with you, and he's gonna make good on it. You better watch yourself." Those seeds found fertile soil in Noble. He'd been trying to figure out a way to strike first without making Tammy mad. Little did he know, Tammy was eager to get rid of Hank, too.

"Hank ain't gonna kill me. I'll kill that bastard first," Noble replied. None of these adults seemed to care who heard them. It was like they didn't think of kids as people who were capable of understanding what they said.

"How you gonna do it?" Tammy asked.

"Depends. You gonna help?"

Tammy said she would. She had some insurance on Hank, and the kids would get Social Security if Hank died, so it made a lot of financial sense. "With him out of the way, we'll be sitting pretty." Tammy gave Noble a wet smack, and they set about planning how to pull it off.

One Saturday, Hank planned on taking his kids to an amusement park. Mama said, "Jackie Lynn, why don't you go with them? Hank is awfully sweet to me, and I think it would be nice if you go and get to know him and his kids."

We had a good day at the amusement park. I even won a stuffed bear shooting a water pistol into a clown's mouth. I liked winning, but I was too big to carry around a stuffed bear, so I gave it to Hank's daughter. Hank drove us back to our house that evening, then picked up Mama to drive with him to drop off Hank's kids at Miz Tammy's house.

That was the day Tammy and Noble decided to strike. They gave Hank and Virginia time to get back home before they put their plan to kill Hank into action. They toasted each other with two shots of Wild Turkey, and off they went.

I saw Noble's green Ford pickup pull into our front yard. Noble hopped out of the truck, nimbler than I expected him to be. I knew something was about to go down. Noble had his hand on his hip as if he was giving final instructions to his .38. That was all I needed to see to get out of the way. I headed down the hall, planning on leaving out the back of the house. Before I could escape, "I heard Mama say, "Don't do this, Noble."

The air always changed when Noble was around. It was thicker, somehow darker, filled with an ominous presence that made the fine blonde hairs on my arms stand at attention. I felt Noble before I saw him. Seconds later, I saw Hank coming from the other direction. In my effort to escape, I had ended up in the middle of two warring bucks. I felt the first bullets whizzing by me. I darted into a bedroom to try to avoid being shot and hid myself in a closet to protect myself further. I sat down on a trunk and prayed to Jesus and my beloved Sylvania to keep me safe, to let me leave this house and enter my Holy of Holies. But not even a sacred space could protect me from this.

I felt a vibration, changing the energy in that dark closet. I didn't realize I'd been shot at first. Adrenaline coursed through my veins and my lizard brain sent me into fight or flight mode. Somehow, I left the closet and saw Noble and Hank on the floor, wrestling over the gun. It wasn't enough to get possession of it, they were each murderous, and when their hands brushed the trigger they pulled, hoping a stray shot would slay the enemy.

I don't think they knew I was there.

Somehow, I made it out of the bedroom, but I didn't make it far. I had lost a lot of blood, though I still didn't know I'd been shot. I blacked out and didn't wake up until I was in a soft, white hospital bed.

I learned later that Hank had the same idea I'd had – that ducking into the bedroom might keep him safe somehow. It didn't: Noble followed right behind Hank into the bedroom, gun blazing. Hank had been shot three times. One of the bullets had gone easily through the extra flesh of his abdomen and through the closet wall. There, it found its way through my arm and into my chest.

I had to have surgery to fix the damage. Thankfully, despite two entry wounds and one exit wound, the worst of it was the loss of blood. It was almost like the bullet had taken a winding path to avoid my bones, major organs, and arteries. The surgeon, a tall man with a shock of black hair and horn-rimmed glasses that reminded me of Superman's, said he'd never seen anything like it. He stood by my bed after I woke up, ruffling my hair like a father on a TV show. "It was as if something was directing the movement of that bullet."

I didn't say anything out loud, but I knew what that something was. It was the hedge of protection that Sylvania had gifted me with before I was born. With her intervention, the bullet traveled in between my radius and my ulna and threaded two ribs, stopping just before entering the right lung. It would take the better part of ten years before I regained full use of my arm. It was a lot of work, but I heard my beloved

Sylvania whispering in my ear, "Where there's a will, there's a way." Since she said it, I knew it was true, and I know I'd been born with plenty of will, so I kept on.

That was forty years ago. The scars have all healed. You'd have to look closely at my body even to see where they were. I rarely feel those tremors that once were a constant reminder of that part of my life.

Chapter Ten

My daughter Chelsea was my firstborn child. From the time she took her first breath, even before, she was everything a parent could dream. Blonde wisps of hair, blue eyes so intense she could see directly into my soul and warm me from the inside. She was too good for this imperfect world.

And so, at eleven, she was diagnosed with a rare form of cancer. My wife and I, along with the head of oncology, had to sit her down and explain to her in very clinical terms just how serious the situation was. She asked, "Am I going to die?" The doctor said, "We are going to do everything we can to give you every chance to live." Chelsea began to interview the doctor, asking the questions her mother and I were too terrified to ask. One of her first concerns was whether there was any chance her sister or brother was in danger of having this cancer. He assured her they were not in danger. Instead of screaming and crying like we were inside our minds, she faced it like the little lady she was, with dignity and grace. She seemed more concerned for her mother and me than herself. Her reassuring tone telling her mother and me "it's going to be okay" haunts me to this day.

Her diagnosis came after a critical bout with high blood pressure. She started chemotherapy, followed by intense radiation. Her beautiful long hair fell out, and most of her meals came roaring back up. But it seemed to be worth it. A final scan showed that the cancer was all gone.

The surgeon shook my hand as if I'd had anything to do with it and said, "It was a miracle."

"We expected that miracle," I said. I'd listened to what the doctors said about her chances, but I knew she'd be held safe by the same hedge of protection that Sylvania had given to me.

"Just as a precaution," the oncologist said, "We'd like to have one more round of chemo, at about 80% potency as we did before, so the side effects shouldn't be as bad."

Given what Chelsea had already been through, this seemed like a small detail, so we agreed. What could go wrong? She'd been through worse.

It was a cold Friday, a few weeks before Christmas. She should be feeling good for the holidays. Our appointment was at a satellite location, not a hospital. We'd been there a year earlier, and we were greeted by unfamiliar faces. Chelsea, an old pro, sat in the chair and waited to be connected to the poison that would make her healthy.

And then, things went wrong. I don't pretend to understand what happened, but it was wrong. After a long night of begging someone to help her, morning came, and an emergency room doctor passed by. Something called him inside her room, and he said, "How long has she been like this?"

"All night."

A sea of white coats and scrubs suddenly surrounded Chelsea. An orderly kicked the locked wheels on her hospital bed and rushed her to the ER. As they rolled her into the elevator, I heard an alarm, and over the intercom: CODE BLUE.

No one would slow down long enough to explain anything to me. Despite the fact that we were in a medical center, I felt the urge to call 9-1-1.

By 7:30 that morning, Chelsea was dead. For most of the next year, my soul fought to follow her. I spent timeless hours in my Holy of Holies, trying to understand why Chelsea would be taken from us so soon after a true miracle.

I battled with God in that place. Like Jacob wrestling with the angel and like Thomas doubting his faith without proof he could touch, I waged an internal war.

The night Chelsea died, she came to me. The next morning, I said to my wife, "Chelsea was in our room last night."

She, too, was skeptical. "How do you know that?

"I could feel her breath on me!"

Over a mug of coffee, my wife looked at me, tears welling in the corner of her eyes.

The next night, I experienced the same thing. Rather than revel in the sweet smell of Chelsea's breath, I opened my eyes. Chelsea stood at our bedroom door. The color that surrounded her rivaled those unearthly colors I'd seen in my Holy of Holies. The air around her was moving. I realized it wasn't her breath but the movement of the air I was feeling. She moved closer to me, into my space, and her aura engulfed me. An understanding beyond human capacity engulfed me. I understood what she understood. I could feel her memories as lively as if I'd experienced them myself. I understood the world as she did.

Without using language spoken by humans, she answered every question I had, even those I couldn't articulate. I saw our beginning and our end and our eventual reunion. For that night, at least, I was filled with peace. I knew she was okay and we would be okay. Despite her death, my beloved Sylvania still protected her.

Chapter Eleven

I received a call from my sister Sue. "Noble's not doing well."

I laughed into the receiver. "Noble's never done well."

"Jack, stop it. You know what I mean."

I did. "Sorry," I mumbled.

"If you want to see him, the doctors are saying he might have a month left."

That led to some serious soul-searching. The only good thing Noble had ever done for me was contribute the genetic material that gave me life. Everything else he'd done or said seemed targeted to make that life more difficult.

Still, he was my father, and without him, I wouldn't be here. I put aside my personal feelings and did what I thought was the right thing to do. I drove to the nursing home where he was living his last days. He sat in a rocking chair on the porch, almost like he was waiting for me.

The scent of Chanel No. 5 was nowhere to be found. The grapevine told me his beloved Tammy had found a new love. I walked up to him, unsure if he would recognize me. It had been years. I guess a father always knows his son, and vice versa. The instant our eyes locked, I knew. I felt a wave of fear and guilt coming off him.

I sat on the edge of the rocker next to him, taking his hand. "Dad. It's good to see you."

"You, too, Jack." It might have been the nicest thing he'd ever said to me. My father, Noble Keeton, was glad to see me. Gone were the days he voiced regret that he hadn't drowned me like a sack of unwanted kittens. This shriveled version of Noble Keeton didn't have the fiery anger in him that plotted murder and hit my mother in the face.

I didn't know what to say, so I chose a topic that was as non-controversial as I could think of. I was still afraid that the Noble I knew would step out of this old man's body and come roaring back to life. "It's a beautiful day. Not too hot, not too cold."

Noble nodded. "Yup. I like to feel the sun on my face. Can't stand being cooped up in a room."

"I'm sure." I fumbled around for another topic. "They feed you well around here?"

"'S'okay." Noble stroked his whiskery chin. "Could stand to use more salt."

We went on in that way for almost an hour. Talking about nothing at all but being together. There was so much I wanted to say to him, and I sensed he was searching for a way to get out of a conversation you'd have with anyone in a grocery store line. We were both scared to go there. There were too many conversational land mines, and neither of us wanted to get hurt any more than we'd already been.

Before I left, I asked, "Would you like me to come back?"

He thought for a moment, then said, "I would like that."

I thought the scars I'd earned having a daddy who didn't want me had healed over, as well as the scars from my bullet wound. But those simple words, letting me know that Noble wanted my company at the end of his life, tore open a hole deep in my soul. I went back every day.

After a couple of weeks of our daily chats about the weather, I finally felt the time was right. I waited for a quiet moment and said, "Dad, I would like to tell you some things."

"So speak, boy." Noble stared off into the middle distance, but I'd learned over the past few weeks that didn't mean he wasn't listening.

"What I have to say isn't meant to hurt you but I need to say it."

Noble readjusted the cannula forcing oxygen into his nose and took a deep breath. "Just say it, Jack. I'm gonna die soon."

I took a deep breath. "I heard you say it more times than I care to remember that you wish you'd killed my bastard ass when I was born. That's a direct quote from you."

Noble made a noise like a deep rumble in his chest that I took for a chuckle. "Well, I didn't, did I?"

"No, you didn't, and even though there were many times I wished you had, I want you to know that I'm grateful you didn't. I've had an amazing life. Believe it or not, some of the things I love most about myself are the parts that are you. I see you every time I look in a mirror. When I'm about to say

94

something that leaves a foul taste in my mouth, because of you, I know how those words will feel, so I don't allow them out. Please don't feel like you weren't enough. You were just what I needed: you were God's version of tough love, and I can only hope I was a part of what you needed in your life experience. I don't need your forgiveness, and you don't need mine. I just want you to see me as I am and not as one of your regrets."

Noble never looked at me as I spoke and never responded in words. He nodded his head and pursed his lips, then went into a long coughing fit that ended with him spitting something bloody into the bushes.

The next morning, I got a call telling me that he had died in his sleep, peacefully.

Conclusion

Not long ago, when I completed my physical therapy, the doctors and insurance company said I was ready for my hip replacement. I was, of course, apprehensive about the surgery even though I knew I needed it. Anesthesia scared me. I have not trusted many people in my life – other than my beloved Sylvania and my beautiful wife, a good number have let me down in their own ways. To go into surgery was to place myself in an unconscious, completely vulnerable place while someone else manipulated my body. The idea scared me.

It wasn't the alternate universe of an anesthetized state that scared me. I'd had a lot of experience disassociating from reality. As a young child, under the stairs in my Holy of Holies, and as I got older on command. I could go to the place where my beloved Sylvania lived in perpetuity, where my angels would sing to me, and where Noble's anger and my mother's neglect had no meaning. This would be different. I couldn't control it.

But living in constant pain, unable to walk where I wanted to wasn't an option. So I prayed the surgeon would treat me well and that I would have a full recovery. A smiling nurse injected my IV with drugs that instantly made me relax and think that this might be okay. When the anesthesiologist put a mask over my face and asked me to count backward from one hundred, her kindly face relaxed me. I don't remember saying any numbers lower than ninety-nine.

I woke up, who knows how much later, to find myself not in a recovery ward but in my Holy of Holies. Surrounding my hospital bed were my angels and my demons alike. All my yesterdays were represented. Like under the stairs, I was in a dimension with no such thing as time. I could communicate with those angels and demons without the limitations of language.

In an instant, I completely understood everything I needed to do, though I couldn't put it in human words. "It's time to wake up," an angel told me. I opened my already-open eyes and found myself sobbing mournfully.

A nurse attendant saw me and patted my shoulder. "It's okay, honey. I'll get the doctor for you."

The anesthesiologist came back, and with the same beatific smile with which she'd sent me off to sleep, she injected something into my IV line. The medicine calmed me down and stopped me from crying, but didn't remove that painful, mournful cry from echoing around my head.

The surgery was perfect. I made a complete recovery, but only physically. That sorrowful sound continued to ricochet around my soul. The voice was familiar. I felt a need, a desire, a longing, but couldn't quite pinpoint what was needed, desired, and longed for. I only knew that it was up to me to do it.

To celebrate my recovery, when I was released from surgery, my wife and I planned a trip to Jamaica. We packed joyfully and hopefully and set off for a place with palm trees and umbrella drinks.

Unfortunately, the voices in my head joined me. As I sat on the white sand beach, staring out over the crystalline Caribbean, my angels and demons begged for relief. I felt like

I had no choice. I settled back under the shade of an umbrella and went to my Holy of Holies.

There, I met the same angels and demons I had encountered in the hospital. They were all clamoring for attention, throwing bits of all my yesterdays at me. To make sense of it, I decided to interview each one, taking down notes. Like playing Clue, I hoped I would be led to the answers as soon as I had enough information.

The youngest of the group stepped forward. He was the only one who actually introduced himself. He didn't say if he was an angel or a demon, and I couldn't tell from looking. He was beautiful, silver-haired, and angelic-looking, but I'd been deceived before. "My name is Sebastian," he said, looking at me with contempt.

"Hello, Sebastian."

Sebastian continued to stare at me, his shining green eyes narrowed and unfriendly.

"May I ask you some questions?"

He shook his head slowly, his rosebud lips pursed into a scowl.

None of the others would speak to me right away. I went through my days functioning, but the longing, the grief, and the sense of desperation overwhelmed me. I felt the pressure of time as if the clocks were running out. We snorkeled in Jamaica, and I had to swim back to shore before the group was finished. I couldn't breathe through that thin tube. I didn't dare try SCUBA diving. Even with a rum runner in my hand and the sun shining on my face on dry land, I felt like I was running out of oxygen. I could see the gauge on the tank; it was dipping fast, and soon, there would be no air, only drowning.

I was determined to set things right. One crystal clear evening, I left my wife in our room and went for a walk on the beach. I perched myself on a rock and closed my eyes. The sound of the surf lulled me, making it easier to quiet my breathing and slip into my Holy of Holies.

As soon as I entered, an angel came to me. "Before you meet the others, I want you to understand who we are. Each of us has had the privilege to accompany you on different parts of your life experience. But on the darkest day of this journey, we were all with you. All of us, including one that is not an angel or demon as you choose to call us. Your beloved Sylvania came to take her great-granddaughter's hand as she let go of her

Daddy's. The following year, we each took turns functioning for you. You spent much of your time in your Holy of Holies. Not even we knew if you would ever come back after the loss of your daughter."

I stared in amazement with my mouth dropped open. When my daughter died, I thought all my spirits had abandoned me. I began to cry, grateful with the sure knowledge that Sylvania had taken her hand from mine that morning she died.

The angel gave me a moment, then said, "Ask how I know you. Ask how you know me."

"How?"

"I was the voice you heard coming from your beloved Sylvania's mouth when she laid hands on your mother's stomach before you were born."

He faded into the background, and a demon stepped forward. I now knew what to say, "How do I know you?"

"I'm the Angel of Darkness that allows you to avoid seeing reality." And, in so, the ability to see everything you needed to see,

Next came another angel. When I asked him the same question, he said, "I composed each piece of music just for you. I created a color for each note."

They each came in their turn, and I asked them how I knew them. "I told Slim every time you were heading to the dumpster."

"I am the spirit of fear. I alerted you before danger approached you so you could escape."

"I was with you the night you were raped. I took your sight so you could not see. I covered your ears so you could not hear the screams coming from your own throat. That night, I knew in the silent darkness, you could find safety."

The next demon that presented himself was bigger than the rest. His face was dark and cloudy. He had black eyes that absorbed all the light around me. I summoned my courage to ask, "How do I know you?"

He laughed a dry, humorless laugh. "I told you to take Noble's thirty-eight out of the gun cabinet. I guided your hands so you could feel the cold, smooth steel. I helped you put it to your head and let you feel the control of God. *Pull the trigger*, I said. *Hear the sound.*"

A blinding flash of light came to me, obliterating the darkness of that demon and replacing it with a surge of hope. "I am here now to show you the consequences your death would bring." A tumble of visions formed in front of me: my grieving wife, my grandchildren, the emptiness of my house, and the hole I'd left. Finally, she showed me a vision of my cousin, Sharon, raising her two daughters alone. "I will be with you just as I am with her."

I thanked the angel. Sharon had been my refuge the summer I was raped. Sharon sheltered me and comforted me. I know without her free-spirited influence, I would have listened to that demon, would have slipped those bullets into Noble's gun, and ended everything right there. I fell to my knees in gratitude: I knew what it felt like to be sheltered by the protection and love of an angel. That Sharon would receive that protection and love as she had protected and loved me was a blessing beyond compare.

The next being that showed itself confused me. Until then, all the beings had been clear to me: angels or demons. They were male or female. This one, however, seemed to transcend such an earthly description. I swallowed thickly and asked, "How do I know you?"

A wind picked up around me. "I am the angel that gave you a voice."

Then, all the beings, the angels, the demons, and the indescribable disappeared, leaving me to think about the gift that the final angel had given me.

Being Noble and Virginia's son, it didn't occur to me to go to college. Book learning was for rich people who didn't have to worry about making a living. I knew it was far better to have a skill that you could use to trade for money. Our high school had a vocational track, where you could graduate from high school and be a certified mechanic or secretary or any number of things. I looked over my choices and decided I wanted to be a barber.

It wasn't so much that I cared about fashion or good looks. But I knew that when you grew up dirty, poor, and unkempt for most of your life, a good haircut could change how people thought about you. There were plenty of boys who wanted to fix cars and plumbing leaks. There'd be a lot of competition for jobs. But not many boys wanted to cut hair.

On my first day of beauty school, fear alerted me the moment I walked into the locker room to change into the white uniform I was expected to wear.

"Do you remember when you opened your locker and looked into the darkness beyond its door?" The angel asked me.

I nodded. "Remember, a peace came over you. That was me."

Oh, I did remember that day. There had to be an angel involved. It felt good to have confirmation. It was a momentous day for me. It was the day I realized I saw my path.

The auto mechanics students also used the locker room. There wasn't a separate locker room for the cosmetology students, and there didn't need to be. I was the first male to attend the program.

I finished the first day confident that I'd made a choice that would propel me into the future I wanted. I walked to my locker to change back into my street clothes. Stripping off my clothes in front of other boys wasn't difficult for me. I was in decent shape and had to do that for gym class my whole life. But this was different. Instead of taking off jeans and a t-shirt and putting on athletic clothes, I was taking off a white shirt, white pants, and a white lab jacket. I caught a glance at myself in the mirror and felt proud. I looked better in those crisp whites than any boy had the right to in a school that more closely resembled a correctional institute.

I thought everyone would be jealous of me. Instead, I heard snickers as I headed towards my locker. A pasty, tall skinny guy whose hairless chest was nearly as white as my uniform called after me, "Pussy."

I could have kept on walking and pretended I didn't hear him or the laughing of the other boys, but I didn't. A ghostly calm surged over me. I paused for a moment and, with all my demons and angels in tow, headed towards that young man. I leaned into him with the calm of the eye of a hurricane. In a voice low enough to be called a whisper and a tone that only a demon could possess, I said, "Have you ever had your ass kicked by a pussy?"

I barely stopped to tell him this, continuing on my way to my locker as if nothing had happened. I stripped down to my underwear, pulled up my worn-out blue jeans, and slipped my Grateful Dead t-shirt over my sun-bleached hair. Still feeling the peace of my heavenly companions, I walked out of that locker room and from that school. My angels and I passed through the stench of stale pot smoke and sweaty teenage angst, leaving behind us a scent that those boys will never forget nor understand.

In that moment, I was determined to have a life beyond the comprehension of the humans that I found myself forced to spend time with in the temporary eternity that is high school. I would have everything I knew they would never have. I would have everything I would allow myself to believe had value.

Of course, even though I thought of myself as a man in those days, I was still only a child. I thought I knew what I wanted and what I valued. I believed I'd have the most beautiful wife, the most beautiful home, perfect children, and the respect of a community. And I would have those things. I am proud of my life and my family, but they weren't everything I wanted or needed. They couldn't heal the wounds I carried that were not physical. Only I could heal those wounds.

There, on that beach in Jamaica, in my Holy of Holies and facing each of my angels and demons in turn, I knew. It would require going back into the belly of my past and coming face to face with each of my scars—the ones that had been inflicted upon me and the self-inflicted ones. The forgiveness and love I sought was that of my own.

I didn't need to apologize to myself. I needed to give myself permission to feel and to be angry. My experience in the locker room showed me that demanding and defending my worth had its own value.

Epilogue

I continue to be haunted by a desperate, nagging need to make right a wrong that I can't quite figure out. I find myself immersing myself in music to drown out the haunts. The melodies seem to soothe my anxiety. I hear the tunes in the still of the night, playing over and over in my head. I think they're a clue.

I have come to an understanding with most of my angels and demons. Sebastian keeps coming to me. He refuses to speak. I know he wants something, and it is completely up to me to figure out what it is. I know in his silence I will hear, and in the darkness I will see. I know the answers lie in the melodies, but I can't read this music. Not yet.

I dream of Sebastian. Asleep, we speak in a language without the limitation of words. I try to come up with crude translations. I don't think about what I'm doing; I just transcribe. When I read what I've written for the first time, I realize Sebastian senses he has been forgotten. He waits and waits for someone to return, but they never do. Eventually, he accepts that he has been forgotten forever.

But he hasn't been. The day I woke up in that recovery room, we both realized he had been locked away in my Holy of Holies, exactly where I had left him.

Sebastian, if you can hear me, know I'm so sorry. I should have believed in you. I thought I was protecting you. I know you had dreams that I never allowed you to pursue. I was the one that was afraid of failure. You had a beautiful voice that I silenced.

I closed my eyes and looked at Sebastian. He was this amazing, beautiful creature. I looked at him, really looked at him for the first time as he stood in silence, his green eyes taking every bit of me in. With a jolt as strong as a lightning bolt, I realized I was staring back at myself.

I am Sebastian. I have been running from myself and something that wasn't chasing me. When speaking to Noble in his last days, I was speaking to myself. My past is my past, and it is right where it belongs. It is behind me, never present. Parts of it were unpleasant or even dangerous, but it was all the components that made me who I am. It deserves to be acknowledged, not forgotten nor ashamed of.

It took all my angels and all my demons to get me to this amazing place of awareness. There is a purpose for every creature that wanders onto your path, angels and demons both. They are all there to teach you something you need. You can learn if you are willing. But you must be willing.

I started writing this book to tell my story of overcoming poverty, abuse, and tragedy to be a person who contributes to the world and sees the beauty in it. After I finished writing, I realized it wasn't a story; it was a revelation to myself. I had written a letter of forgiveness, the gift of permission, an offering of love.

Sometimes, we run so fast that we aren't even aware of what's happening in the moment. The scenery blurs by. After finishing the last word, I went to bed and slept like I don't think I've ever slept before. I dreamed I went to the Performing Arts Center with my beautiful wife and our precious children. We were seated and watched the orchestra settle itself and tune up. The conductor came to the stage, riding a wave of thunderous applause. He tapped his baton on a music stand, then lifted it. When he began to conduct, the orchestra sang.

Immediately, I recognized that the orchestra was playing the music from my Holy of Holies. It was the nameless tune that played the first time I'd heard it, and it filled the space under the stairs.

When the concert ended, the lights went up, and the curtain went down. But the show wasn't over. The heavy velvet drapes of the curtain parted one last time, and all the amazing characters in my life came out for their final bow. My beloved Sylvania was there, as was my mother and Noble. My daughter, who had left me all those years ago. Mrs. Bentley gave a gracious curtsy. They all, hand in hand, parted in the center to make room for one last performer. From out of the shadows, a small presence appeared. It was Sebastian; he looked so small as he came out of the shadows to reach the spotlight center stage as a grown man appeared not afraid to join the cast and take his much-deserved place alongside me. Good and bad, angel and demon. I was so proud of their courage. Each of them had done a perfect job in shaping the clay that was to become me. It wasn't until that moment that I realized how beautifully broken we all must be to fit so perfectly into each other's lives.

A life well lived is one that you can look back on and see beauty in the ashes. I know without hesitation I would do it all again and not change a thing because it all happened just the way it was meant to be. Sometimes, the ending is just the beginning.

I have been lucky.

THE END

About the Author

Jack Keeton currently lives in the same town in Ohio where his family migrated to in the early 1950s from Elliott County, Kentucky.

His children and grandchildren live within walking distance of him and his wife of 42 years. His wish is that you see beauty in the ashes as he has learned to. This book was a work of love and discovery, and yes, in bringing you a story, obviously, the dialogue is fiction, but the content is based on his journey and recollections as a child!

In the words of the great Maya Angelou, people will forget what you said, but never forget the way you made them feel! Speak love, kindness, and inspiration into your children! And never forget the love of our family who came before us and lined the paths we find ourselves on!

This book is a short read by design. I have learned that too many words can distract from what you wish to say. The picture above was taken on the Simon Kenton bridge that Jack's family would have crossed from Kentucky to Ohio. In many ways, it was much like immigrants from Europe who left the only way of life they knew behind for the hope of a better life.

Printed in Great Britain
by Amazon